# CLOSE TO HOME

## Oralee Wachter

### Illustrated by Jane Aaron

## SCHOLASTIC INC.
New York  Toronto  London  Auckland  Sydney

*For Natalie*
*and her friends*

ISBN 0-590-40331-1

12 11 10 9 8 7 6 5 4 3 2 1          10          6 7 8 9/8 0 1/9

Printed in the U.S.A.

# Introduction

WHAT if a person tells you to do something that doesn't feel safe? What do you do? What if someone wants you to get into a car and go somewhere that you're not sure it's okay to go? What do you say? Should you or shouldn't you?

It's always safer to stick with your friends, stay with the group, and keep out of dangerous places. You probably know better than to go anywhere in a car with a stranger. But what if a stranger acts friendly, and makes you feel mixed-up? What if someone you know and trust wants you to go somewhere you don't want to go? When that happens, it's hard to know what to do.

These stories are about kids like you, who may not know what the safe thing is to do. This book can help you practice taking care of yourself by showing you all sorts of different situations with different kinds of people. Above all, it's about learning to feel and be safe — at school, at home, wherever you may be.

# Super Safe

Janie's mother worked at home in her office upstairs. She had a sign on the door that said Do Not Disturb Till _____. The sign had a small clock on it with hands that moved. After they had lunch together, Janie walked her mom to the office. She liked to fix the hands of the clock to say five o'clock and hang the sign on the doorknob.

"Bye, Mom," said Janie. "Have a good day at the office."

"I will. Remember the rules?" asked her mother.

"Number one, no interruptions, unless it's super important. Number two, don't go anywhere without asking first. And number three, Pam's in charge," answered Janie.

"Right," said her mom. She gave Janie a kiss

good-bye. "If I finish my work early, I'll meet you and Pam at the playground."

Pam was Janie's baby-sitter. She was drying the lunch dishes when Janie came downstairs. They read the list of errands Janie's mother had left for them to do:

Pick up cleaning
Store — choc. bits, brown sugar, eggs,
low-fat milk, bananas

"Looks like we're going to make Tollhouse cookies today," said Pam.

"Let's not put any nuts in them this time, okay?" said Janie.

"They're not real Tollhouse cookies if they don't have nuts," said Pam.

"I don't care. I like them better that way," Janie said.

Janie and Pam were getting ready to go to the store when the doorbell rang. It was Pam's boyfriend, Gary. He came over to show Pam his new truck.

"Want to go for a ride in my new pickup?" he

asked. "I'll take both of you for a ride around the block."

"We have to go to the store," said Pam, "and then to the playground."

"I'll drive you. Come on. It's a great car. You'll love it," said Gary.

Janie wanted to go. She wasn't sure if it was okay. "Let's go ask Mom," she said.

"No, we're not supposed to interrupt, remem-

ber?" answered Pam. "Gary's a friend of mine. I'm sure she won't mind. Let's go."

The three of them sat up front and Gary drove out to the beach, past the store and the playground. His dog, Keats, was scrambling from side to side in the back of the truck. Gary's truck didn't have a seat belt for Janie, so she could look out the back window and watch Keats. He looked funny with his hair and ears blowing in the wind. Janie forgot all about meeting her mom.

When Janie's mom got to the playground, it was late. Only Russell and Sophie were still playing on the swings.

"Where's Janie?" she asked them.

"Janie's not here," said Russell.

Janie's mom looked upset. She walked over to the bench where Russell's mother was sitting.

"Have you seen Janie and Pam?" she asked.

"No, they haven't been here today," said Russell's mother.

"That's funny," said Janie's mom. "I said I might meet them here. I wonder where they are."

She looked for them all around the playground

and in the Nature Center. *I wonder what could have happened to them*, she thought. She walked home as fast as she could. They were not there. She looked on the kitchen table to see if Pam had left a note telling her where they had gone. No note. Janie's mother began to worry about all kinds of things that might have happened. Maybe they had a serious accident. She called the hospital. No little girl had been taken to the hospital. Maybe they got lost. She was ready to call the police department.

Just then the door opened, and Janie and Pam walked in carrying a bag of groceries.

"Hi, Mom," said Janie. "We went for a ride in Gary's new truck, with Keats."

Janie's mom was glad they were home safe. She was so happy to see them she smiled and hugged Janie and gave her a big kiss. Then she remembered all the dangerous things that might have happened to them, and she stopped smiling. She looked very serious.

"Who's Gary?" she asked Pam and Janie. "Who's Keats? Who gave you permission to get into a truck? Why didn't you go to the playground like you were supposed to? Didn't you know I'd be worried about you?" she asked all at once.

Pam tried to explain. "I guess it was my fault," she said. "Gary's a friend of mine. I thought it would be okay to go for a ride with him. I know Gary real well."

"I know him, too," said Janie. "He's really nice. And I love Keats."

"I'm glad he's nice. That's great. But I don't know him," said Janie's mom. "And that's the point. You're not allowed to go anywhere with a person I don't know. It's as simple as that. Always ask me first. Don't go anywhere without my permission. No surprises. That's a rule."

"We didn't want to interrupt you, Mom," said Janie.

"That's a rule, too, isn't it?" asked Pam. "No interruptions unless it's important."

"Nothing is more important than being safe. It's *super* important," answered Janie's mom. "I have to know where Janie is and who she is with all the time. Both of you have to follow the rules so I know you're safe…*super* safe, even when I'm not with you."

The next day after lunch, Janie took her mom to the office as usual. Janie set the hands of the clock at five o'clock and hung the sign on the doorknob.

"Mom, are you still mad at Pam and me?" asked Janie.

"It's not that I'm mad. I'm worried. I'm afraid you and Pam don't know what the rules are," she answered.

"But I do know. Number one, I can't go anywhere with a person my mom doesn't know. Number two, Pam's in charge. Number three, if I'm not sure, I can always call or knock on the door to find out if it's okay. Right?"

"Right," said her mother. "Now I feel better."

Janie thought about it for a minute. Then she asked, "If we bake cookies today, and Pam wants nuts in them and I don't, should I knock on the door and ask you what to do?"

Her mom gave her a hug. "Is that super important?" asked her mother.

"Sort of," said Janie, teasing.

"Okay. How about half with nuts, and half without?" suggested her mom.

"Good idea," said Janie. "Have a good day at the office, Mom."

"Have a good day with Pam," answered her mother, smiling.

# Shortcut

PAUL didn't have to hear the bell ring to know he was late. The halls were empty, as if a giant magnet had pulled everyone off the playground, into their classrooms, and slammed the doors shut. *Not again*, he thought. *I better have a good excuse.*

Mrs. Schaffer looked up from her desk when Paul opened the door. She took out the roll book and put a check mark next to his name. "Late again," she said. "What happened this time?"

Everyone stopped what they were doing to hear one of Paul's "long stories" about why he was always late. "Did the dog eat your homework?" yelled out his friend Chip. Everyone giggled.

"Well, it's a long story..." he began. Mrs. Schaffer motioned time-out with her hands. That meant stop.

"I'll have plenty of time to listen after school, Paul. Get started on your workbook now."

"I can't stay today. I have hockey practice after school," said Paul. "Coach is choosing the team to play in the league. If I'm late again he'll drop me."

Mrs. Schaffer was not impressed. "We'll talk about it after school."

At three o'clock the bell rang. Paul watched his friends go off to hockey practice with their sticks and skates. In a few minutes they would be speed-

ing over the ice, while he was going to be stuck in school with Mrs. Schaffer forever.

At three-thirty she let him go, and Paul dashed out the door. If he wasn't on the ice by four o'clock sharp, his coach made him sit on the bench for the whole practice. *I'll never make it. It's probably four o'clock already. What a day this is turning out to be.* He hurried down the street toward the skating rink.

The safest way to get there was through the shopping mall, then down ten more long blocks. The fastest way was to take the shortcut. Paul thought about it for a minute. The shortcut was through a vacant lot full of weeds and bushes and junk. Nobody was supposed to go in. There was a fence around it to keep people out, but someone had cut and twisted it down to the ground in a couple of places.

Paul knew the shortcut was off limits. All the kids did. But they didn't believe strange things happened there. Paul and his friends had raced through it together lots of times. First, they'd make a lot of noise whooping and roaring to scare away

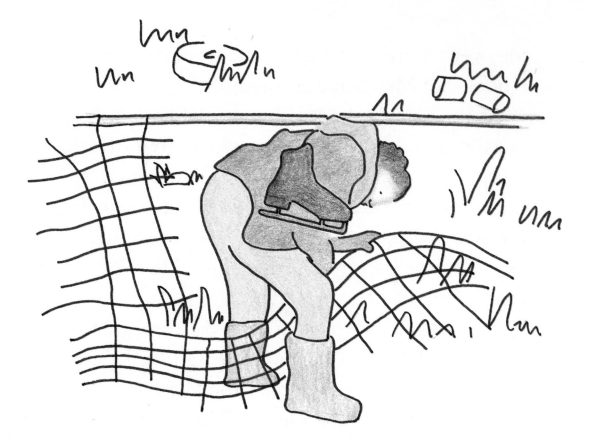

anyone who might be lurking in the bushes. Then they'd skip over the empty cans and dodge around piles of junk, practicing hockey moves as they ran.

Paul stood by the hole in the fence behind the supermarket where the huge trucks unloaded. He put his foot on the rusted wires. He had never taken the shortcut by himself. The place looked kind of scary in the late afternoon shadows. He wished his friends were there to make him feel braver. *Should I or shouldn't I?* he asked himself.

Paul zipped his jacket all the way up and stepped over the fence. He could see the flat roof of the skating rink in the distance as he started to walk quickly through the tangled weeds. *This isn't so bad*, he thought. *I'll be there in a couple of minutes.* He sidestepped an old broken car seat, and continued on his way. "This is no big deal," he said out loud. "This isn't scary or anything. No problem."

*I bet everyone is suited up by now. They're probably just hitting the ice.* He walked a little faster, thinking about how much he wanted to make the team. *I hope Coach isn't mad at me. I better think of an excuse for being late to practice.* Paul had gone more than halfway, when he saw a man step out of the bushes up ahead.

"Hey, you there," the man called out. "What are you doing in here?"

Paul stopped on the spot. The sun was setting. All he could see was the shape of a tall man wearing a hat. He couldn't see the man's face in the shadow of the hat. His heart was suddenly beating very fast.

"You're not supposed to be here. This is private property," said the man. Paul could see the man's breath steam up in the cold air. "Come with me."

The man took a few steps toward him, getting closer and closer. Paul wanted to run, but for a moment, he couldn't move. His legs felt like wooden poles stuck in the ground. He felt sweaty inside his jacket.

"What do you mean?" said Paul. "Where are we going?"

"Stay right there," said the man. He pointed

to a van parked on the other side of the field. "I'm going to take you home before you get into trouble."

The man kept walking slowly toward him. He was almost close enough to touch, when he reached out to grab Paul's arm. Paul jumped back. He ducked to the side, spun around, and ran. He headed straight for the hole in the fence and the safety of the supermarket, jumping over the weeds and broken bottles on the way. He didn't know if the man was chasing him or not. He was afraid to look back. He kept running through the parking lot, past the loading dock, and around to the front of the store. The automatic doors swung open and he ran inside.

His heart was pounding so loud he could hear it. He flopped down on a stack of dog food bags in front of the checkout counter to catch his breath. He sat there for a long time, watching for the man through the glass storefront. There was no sign of him.

As soon as he was sure the man was nowhere in sight, Paul began to calm down. When he felt better, he walked slowly to hockey practice. It took a long time. It was almost dark when he got there. He could hear the voices of his teammates and the sound of their skates and hockey sticks scraping on the ice. It was too late to bother putting on his uniform. Paul sat down and watched the game. At halftime the coach noticed him sitting on the bench.

"Paul, I see you finally got here. What took you so long?" he asked.

"It's a long story, Coach," said Paul. His voice was small and shaky.

"What's the matter, Paul?" said the coach. "You look like you need a friend."

"You wouldn't believe me if I told you," said Paul.

"Try me," said the coach. "Tell me what happened."

"Well," said Paul, "first I was late to school. Then I had to stay after school 'cause I was late getting there. And that made me late to hockey. So, I took a shortcut. I cut across that deserted lot by the supermarket."

"Don't you know that place isn't safe?" asked the coach.

"Yeah, but I did it anyway," said Paul. "I was walking along, when this man came out of nowhere. He acted like a guard, but I don't think he really was. He tried to grab me and put me in his van."

"What did you do?" asked the coach.

"I just took off. I ran away from him. That's why I didn't get here on time," said Paul. "This is probably the worst day of my life."

"I wouldn't say that," said the coach. "I'd say this was your lucky day. You were *very* lucky to get away."

"Yeah, but maybe he really was a security guard," said Paul.

"I doubt it. It sounds like he was trying to scare you into going with him. It's a good thing you didn't let him talk you into it," answered the coach.

"But if he *was* the police, or someone like that, I'll be in trouble," said Paul.

"No you won't," said the coach. "If he was the police, he'll understand. He'll know you were looking out for yourself and being careful. Getting out of there was absolutely the right thing to do."

Paul put his head down on the bench. "I wish I had been here. Then none of this would have happened," said Paul.

"True," said the coach. "But you learned something important today. Don't go off by yourself. Stick with your friends. Stay with the group. And keep out of places that aren't safe."

"I guess I didn't make the team," said Paul.

"I wouldn't say that either," said the coach. "You were quick on your feet. You used good judgment and got out of a tight spot. I can always use a player like that. You get here on time tomorrow, and I'll give you another chance to try out for the team."

Paul sat up, feeling much better. "I'll be here," he said. "Four o'clock sharp." He watched the rest of the game from the bench. When it was over, Paul and his friends took the long way home, down the safe, familiar streets they knew, together.

# Girl Friends

THE only thing Gina and Kim had in common was living at the top of Hillcrest Road, the steepest, longest, hardest hill in the whole city. Even cars had a hard time going up that hill. Every day since the first grade they had walked home together, zigzagging up the seven long blocks to the top. Gina was the tallest girl in the sixth grade. Kim was the second shortest. Gina had two sisters. Kim had two brothers. Gina wore lots of lipstick, read romance novels, and saved her money to buy clothes. Kim wore any old thing, loved science fiction, and wanted to be the class president. They were best friends.

Halfway up the hill Gina and Kim turned around and walked backward to give their tired legs a rest. It also gave them a clear view of any car

that was coming up the hill. When they saw someone they knew, like a neighbor or one of Kim's
brothers, Gina would stick out her thumb and beg
for a ride to the top of the hill. Sometimes it
worked.

"Do you think Ned Tully is nice?" asked Gina.

"No. Definitely not. He's always showing off,"
said Kim.

"I think he's cute," said Gina.

"You think everyone's cute," said Kim.

"I do not."

"What about Brian?" asked Kim. "I thought you
liked him."

"We're friends. He's okay," said Gina.

"I think he's dumb," said Kim.

"You think everyone's dumb," said Gina.

"I do not!" they both said at the same time.
They walked backward up the hill without saying
a word to each other, until Gina noticed a blue car
climbing slowly up the hill, getting closer and
closer.

"Here comes a car," said Gina. "I want a ride."

"Is it someone we know?" asked Kim hopefully.

"It's too far away. I can't tell," said Gina, squinting her eyes at the car.

When the car finally made it up to them, it stopped, and a young man wearing a T-shirt waved to them. He stuck his head out of the window and called out.

"Hi," he said. "Do you girls know where Mountain View Road is?"

"Mountain View? Sure. It's two more blocks straight up the hill," Gina told him.

"Great. Thanks a lot. Are you going that way?" he asked.

"Yeah. We go all the way to the top," said Gina.

"Well, get in, and I'll drive you," said the man.

"No. That's okay," said Kim. "We can walk."

"Are you sure?" he said. "It's a long hill."

Gina looked at Kim. "C'mon, let's get in. I will if you will," she said.

"You go ahead if you want to," said Kim. "I'm walking."

"I guess I'll walk," Gina said to him.

"Okay. Whatever you say. Maybe I'll see you around again some time." He stuck his arm out the

window and waved as he drove up the hill. Gina waved back.

"Why'd you say no?" complained Gina. "Now we have to walk up this humongus hill."

"Didn't you ever hear about not talking to strangers?" said Kim.

"He wasn't that kind of a stranger. He wasn't a weirdo or anything," said Gina.

"What if he didn't want to let us out of the car?" asked Kim. "Then what?"

"Well, you didn't have to be so mean to him," said Gina.

"You didn't have to be so nice to him, either," said Kim. She turned around and started to walk forward up the hill.

Gina turned around, too. "I was just being friendly," she said. "I thought you were the one who liked to be *sooooo* friendly to everyone."

"That's different. Those are my friends. Not some man I don't even know, who tries to pick up two girls. He gave me a creepy feeling," said Kim.

"He wasn't a man. He wasn't any older than your brother," said Gina. "I think he was cute."

"You would," said Kim.

"You act like such a baby sometimes," said Gina. "I wish you'd just grow up."

Kim didn't answer. They walked silently to the top of the hill. Then Kim turned to the right and Gina turned to the left. They didn't say, "So long," or "See you," like they usually did.

The next day Kim was still mad. She started up the hill alone. It seemed even longer and steeper without someone to talk to. *Even arguing with*

*Gina is better than this,* she thought.

Then she saw the same blue car parked up ahead. The man in the T-shirt was standing there, leaning against the open door. *What's he want now?* she wondered. *He can't be lost again.*

"Hi," he said. "Remember me?"

Kim ignored him.

"Want a ride?" he asked.

"No," she answered. Kim crossed the street to get away from him. She turned around and walked backward to see what he was going to do next.

"Where's your friend?" he asked.

Kim just ignored him.

*None of your business,* she thought to herself. Then Kim saw Gina walking up the hill toward the blue car. She wondered if Gina would be dumb enough to get into the car with him.

Gina stopped when she got to the car. Kim could see them talking. Then she saw the man put his hand on Gina's shoulder. It gave Kim that creepy feeling about him again. She started to run down the hill toward Gina.

"Geeeennnah!" called Kim. It was hard to keep from going too fast. "Wait a second."

Gina looked up and saw Kim running downhill at full speed. She almost crashed right into them.

"What do you want?" said Gina. "What's wrong?"

Kim didn't know exactly what to say. She just knew she didn't want Gina getting into the car with that man.

"C'mon, Gina," said the man. "Let's go." He kept his hand on Gina's shoulder and pulled her a little closer to him.

Kim grabbed Gina's other arm.

"Don't, Gina," said Kim. "We're walking."

Gina looked at Kim. "I guess I better not," Gina said to the man.

"C'mon, honey," he said. "There's nothing to be afraid of."

"Don't answer him," said Kim. "Let's just go home, Gina, please."

"Don't listen to her. She's just a kid," he said to Gina. "Let's go." He took Gina's arm and tried to pull her into the car.

"Hey! Let go of her," Kim yelled. Gina pulled her arm away and stood next to Kim. "Just leave us alone," Kim went on yelling. "I told my father about you. I took your license number. He's going to report you to the police. You better get out of here."

"Don't get so excited," said the man. "I was just going to drive your friend home. Right, Gina?"

Gina was too scared to answer him. She and Kim crossed the street and watched the blue car drive up the hill. He didn't wave good-bye this time.

"I'm sorry I said all that stuff yesterday," said Gina.

"Me, too," said Kim.

"Did you really give his license number to your father?" asked Gina.

"No. But I told my mom that you and I had a fight about that guy. She said to get his license number if he ever bothered us again."

"Are you going to tell her?" asked Gina.

"Yeah, I guess so," said Kim. "Maybe she'll call the police and have them check the guy out. My mom does things like that."

"What good will that do?" asked Gina.

"I don't know. Maybe he hangs around schools and tries to pick up other kids dumb enough to get into his car."

"Do you think he was trying to kidnap me or something?" said Gina.

"Probably. If I hadn't saved you," said Kim.

"I wasn't really going to get into his car," said Gina.

"You were, too," said Kim.

"I was not!" they both said together. Then they laughed and turned around to walk up the hill backward the rest of the way home.

# Close to Home

Terrie was surprised to see her dad waiting in the car after school one day. It was right in the middle of the week, before Thanksgiving vacation. She didn't expect to see him until Saturday.

Terrie ran over to the car. "Daddy, how come you're here today?" she said.

"Hop in, Terrie," said her father. "We're going to pick up your brother. I've got a surprise for both of you."

"How come?" asked Terrie. "It's Wednesday."

"That's okay," answered Mr. Phillips. "You'll see. Get in."

They drove to Marshall Junior High to pick up Jeff. While they waited for the bell to ring, Terrie wondered what the surprise could be. Ever since her parents were divorced she only saw her father every other weekend. Her mother was very strict about that. If her dad called and said, "Can I pick

35

up the kids tomorrow and take them to a ball game?" her mother always answered, "No. We made an agreement about that, Jack. Let's just stick to the agreement."

Before "the agreement" they used to argue all the time about who Terrie and Jeff should live with. "They're my children and I love them," said her mother. "I want them to live with me."

"They're my children, too, and I love them just as much as you do," said her father. "I want them to live with me."

Finally, her mother and father went to court and a judge made them agree to take turns. She said they were supposed to live with their mother most of the time, and every other weekend they could stay with their father at his house. That's what they always did.

In a few minutes the school bell rang and Jeff came out of the gym carrying his skateboard. When he saw his father he was just as surprised as Terrie had been.

"Hey, Dad, what's up?" said Jeff. "You're not supposed to pick us up today, are you?"

"Get in, Jeff. I'll tell you all about it in the car," answered his father.

"Okay," said Jeff, "but does Mom know you're here?"

His father didn't answer. "Jeff, you're making us late. Hurry up."

"I'm coming," said Jeff. He got in the car and put his skateboard on the backseat.

"Okay, Daddy. Now tell us, where are we going?" said Terrie.

"Yeah, and how come we're in such a big hurry?" asked Jeff.

"You'll see. It's a surprise," said their father.

"What kind of surprise?" said Jeff.

"A big one. How does Disney World sound to you?" said their father.

"It sounds great. But it's in Florida, Dad," said Jeff.

"Florida? Well, I guess that's where we'll have to go, then," he said.

"Are you just kidding around, Dad?"

He handed Jeff a folder of airline tickets. "Take a look, Jeff. See if they say Disney World on them."

Jeff opened the folder and took out the airline tickets. "Disney World," he read. "You mean we're going right now?"

"Why not? We've got four whole days for Thanksgiving, and I thought we should do something really different. We're going to have a great time."

"But we always go to Aunt Sally's for Thanksgiving," said Jeff.

"Well, this year is different," Mr. Phillips answered. "This year we're going to be together."

Terrie had a funny feeling right then and there. "Did Mom say I could go, too?"

"Of course she did," said Mr. Phillips.

That didn't sound like her mom at all. "Are you sure?" asked Terrie.

"I said she did, didn't I?" answered her father.

"How come you two are so suspicious?" he asked. "I'm your father. Can't I take you on a trip?"

"Sure," said Jeff. "But how come Mom didn't tell us about it?"

"Maybe she didn't want to spoil the surprise. You both sound like I'm kidnapping you, or something," said their father.

"What's kidnapping?" asked Terrie.

"That's when someone takes you away, and doesn't bring you back," said Jeff. "I saw it on TV. They showed pictures of kids who never got to go back home. And their parents keep on looking for them all over the country."

"What about our clothes and stuff?" asked Terrie.

"I already thought of that, and I put some of your things in the trunk. Anyway, we don't need much down there. If we need anything, we can buy it when we get there. Right?" asked her father.

"Yeah, I guess so," said Terrie.

"Now, will you two stop worrying?" asked their father.

"It just seems funny," said Jeff. "Not saying good-bye to Mom."

"If you don't want to go," said their father, "I'll turn around right now. I thought it was a great idea. But if you'd rather stay home, all you have to do is say so. I know plenty of kids who'd love to go to Disney World."

Terrie and Jeff didn't say anything for the rest of the ride to the airport. Terrie knew she wasn't supposed to go anywhere with anyone without her mother's permission. Her mom always made her promise to call home and check in if she was going to be late or anything like that. But this was different. Being with her father didn't count. Did it?

Terrie wondered if her mom was worried about them. Then her mother would be mad at her father and they'd get into a big fight. Terrie hated it when they got into arguments about her and Jeff.

"Daddy," said Terrie, "when we get to the airport, I'm going to call Mom. I want to tell her something, okay?"

"We're not going to have time for that, Terrie," said her father. "It's getting late and I don't want us to miss the plane."

"But I want to talk to her," said Terrie. Her eyes were filling with tears.

"We have plenty of time," said Jeff. "The tickets said the plane leaves at five-thirty. You can call Mom, Terrie. Don't worry about it."

"Promise?" said Terrie.

"I promise," said her father, "but only if we have enough time."

The airport was crowded with people going away for the holiday. They had to stand in long lines and wait their turn to check in and get their seats on the plane.

"We want three seats together in the No Smoking Section," said Mr. Phillips.

"Can I call Mom now?" asked Terrie.

"Not now," said her father.

He took Terrie's hand firmly and led her to the security check-in. They waited in another long line while all the passengers were checked to be sure nothing dangerous was taken onto the plane.

"Can I call now?" asked Terrie.

"No," said her father. He looked angry. "I go to all this trouble to give you a good time. I've spent a lot of money, too. And all I get from both of you is a lot of questions. I don't want to hear another word about your mother."

Mr. Phillips took them to the snack bar and ordered french fries and lemonade. "I'm going to get some magazines. I want you two to sit here and eat your fries," he said. "We'll be getting on the plane in a couple of minutes."

Jeff and Terrie sat at the table and stared at their fries. "Jeff, how come Daddy won't let me call home?" said Terrie.

"I don't know," said Jeff. "Something's wrong."

"Mom's going to be so mad at me. She says, 'Always call. You're never too busy to call home,'" said Terrie sadly.

Jeff remembered the pictures of kids he'd seen on TV — the ones who went off with someone and couldn't get home again.

"Maybe we better not go," said Jeff.

"But he'll feel real bad," said Terrie, "like we don't want to be with him."

"I know, but if he's taking us away without Mom's permission, she'll feel bad, too," said Jeff. "We'll be in trouble no matter what we do."

Their father came back with bubble gum and magazines. "Hey, come on, you kids haven't eaten anything."

"I'm not hungry," said Jeff.

"Not hungry for french fries? What's wrong?" asked his father. "Are you sick?"

"No," said Jeff. He poked at the soggy fries with his finger. "I just don't want them." Then he pushed the plate away. "I don't want to go to Disney World, either," Jeff blurted out. "I don't believe you. I don't think Mom said we could go."

"Jeff, that's enough. I'm your father and when you're with me you'll do as I say."

"Why won't you let Terrie call Mom? She just wants to say good-bye." Now Jeff was almost in tears, too. "You're just trying to trick us into going. You're going to get us all in trouble."

Mr. Phillips frowned. "I'll take the blame. Nobody's going to get in trouble. I'll call your mother myself when we get there. There's nothing to worry about."

"But that's not fair!" said Jeff. "We have to do what you say and we have to do what Mom says, too. How are we supposed to do both? I don't want to go to Disney World. It won't be any fun like this."

"Is that how you feel, Terrie?" asked her father. "Are you going to let me down, too?"

Terrie nodded her head.

"I'm disappointed in both of you, but I guess there's no point in going," he said. "I'll just return the tickets and forget about the whole thing."

When Terrie and Jeff got home their mother was very upset. She was mad at their father. Their father was mad at both of them. They felt mixed-up about the whole thing.

Their mother and father stood on the lawn, yelling at each other. Terrie and Jeff went upstairs.

This is what always happened. A little while later Mrs. Phillips came upstairs.

"I'm so glad both of you are home, safe and sound," said their mother. She put her arms around them and hugged them tight. "Are you sure you're okay?"

"Yes. We're fine," said Jeff. "Nothing happened. Dad just wanted to take us on a vacation."

"He knows he should have asked me," said their mother.

"You always say no!" said Jeff.

"Now you're mad at Dad, aren't you?" asked Terrie.

"Of course I am," she answered. "I didn't know where you were. I've been worried about you all afternoon. Your father has no right to take you away without discussing it with me first. It's against the law."

"Against the law? What do you mean?" asked Jeff.

"When your dad and I were divorced, we signed an agreement. That's like a promise. We agreed that when you're with either one of us the other parent has to know where you are, and has to say it's okay. Breaking that promise is like breaking the law. It's very serious."

"What's going to happen?" asked Jeff. "Is Dad in trouble?"

"I don't know. I'm angry at your father because he broke his promise, and he nearly broke the law. I want to make sure that nothing like this ever happens again. But I want you to know I'm proud of both of you. I'm sure you were very confused. I know it was hard, but you did the right thing."

That night in her own bed, Terrie felt better. She was disappointed, but she was glad she was safe at home. She wished the trip to Disney World had turned out differently. She wished her father had planned the trip the right way. She wished her mother had said she could go and had helped her pack a suitcase. She even imagined her mother smiling and waving good-bye at the door. Terrie snuggled down under the covers. She hoped that next time it would be like that.